W9-CUK-648

A Collection of Short Stories

by Gary Carter

ISBN: 978-1-931002-77-6

Wordrunner Press
Petaluma, California

Dedicated to the women who have filled my
life and let me think I knew what I was doing;
with deepest gratitude to my wonderful wife
Harriet, without whom these words could
not have been processed, and to our amazing
daughters Cathy, Rachel, Jennifer, and Tamala,
all of them experts at making life work.

Acknowledgments

To Judith Stephensen, Guy Biederman, Floyd Beaver, Elliot Joseph, and Leif Calvin for their support and advice.

With special gratitude to Jo-Anne Rosen of Wordrunner Press for her expertise and taste as she built this book.

CONTENTS

Max and Charley

Max Dorfman pressed his back against the smooth wide boards of the old Adirondack chair and carefully straightened his right leg until it was almost parallel to the ground. He held it up for a moment, then eased it down again. The blue summer morning, chilly in its earliness, was warming a little now as the sun lifted clear of the feather-tipped fir trees across the road and soaked into Dorfman's eighty-year-old body. His brown-spotted hands, large and slack skinned, rested sphinx-like on the arms of the weathered wooden seat.

He smiled and nodded a greeting as Charley Johnson, almost as old as Max and equally as work-worn, settled into the adjacent chair. Charley was powerfully built, heavy-necked, solid. The two men were relaxed in each others' company, with or without words. They knew each others' lives, respected and enjoyed one another, and spent the major part of each day nested here on the quiet, sagging porch of Max's house.

Both men had spent their lives working as skilled craftsmen in the nearby city; Max as a cabinetmaker building beautiful things out of walnut and clear white oak, Charley as a bricklayer — fast, accurate, strong, and proud of the churches and monuments that would bear the soul of Charley long after he was gone.

Their conversation was simple, considered, and sparse. Extended silences were taken as opportunities to study the occasional passing pickup truck or to rub the crick out of one's neck.

～

A large, dark bird launched itself from the top of the tallest fir tree and pumped off toward the woods to the east. Both men watched as the slicing silhouette grew smaller until it was gone. The only sound was a jay calling from behind the house and the creak of Charley's chair as he withdrew his gaze from the distant woods and leaned back thoughtfully.

"Sparrow hawk," he said. A gentle breeze moved the high branches in silence.

Max leaned back and both men watched the tops of the fir trees.

"Maybe a red-tail."

Three minutes slipped by.

"Maybe."

And quiet thoughtfulness reigned once again.

～

This is not to say that Max and Charley never disagreed.

One morning in late September when the sun was beginning to drift off to the south with the season, the angle of the light across the wide arm of Max's chair caused him to focus on a glue-joint he had never noticed before; a gray line in the dark brown wood. Summoning Charley's attention with a downward nod, he ran his finger along the line.

"Lousy glue job."

Charley squinted and leaned a few degrees closer. "Looks okay from here."

"It's lousy," Max insisted. "Not enough clamp. You shouldn't be able to see the glue line. You can see the goddamned glue holding the boards apart."

Charley adjusted his feet, pulled out a pair of reading glasses, and took another look. Max's finger still rested on one end of the line. "Seems to me like it's the glue that's holding the boards *together*."

Max sat back for a minute, thinking. "No," he decided, "If they was together they'd be touching each other. That's the problem. The goddamned glue's holding 'em apart."

Charley looked up and out at the green across the road. Spinning red dust jumped up behind a truck as it rattled past. The driver waved. When quiet had settled in again, Charley looked back down at the problem, frowning. A schoolteacher-emphasis crept into his voice. "Without the glue, the boards wouldn't stay together now, would they?" Max hesitated for a moment so Charley pressed on. "So it must be the goddamned glue that's holding them together!"

"No, if they was together, there wouldn't be anything be-tween 'em," Max countered.

"You're saying," Charley asked, striving for clarity, "that the boards have to be touching to be together?"

"Damn right." The woodworker had spoken.

Charley pondered for a moment, then looked across at his old friend, straight into his face. "Let me ask you something," he said. "Don't we sit here together every single day?"

"Well... yeah."

"And have we ever touched each other?"

"Hell no!"

"Well, okay then."

Max looked straight ahead.

"Wood's different," he said quietly.

The Boston Señora

Many years have passed since I was in Cerritos, but as I remember it, the hill rose above the little Mexican town like a steep volcanic island thrust above a sea of yellow sand. As a young man, I recall coaxing my reluctant body up the dusty path, dreading the ordeal that awaited me at the top; a visit with Señora Corego.

Where the village faded into the face of the slope, stone steps had been carved out of the rocky hillside and curved upward beside a dry stone wall to a tiled landing indented like an afterthought into one corner of the Señora's boxy stucco house.

Her front door loomed at the end of the landing and a concrete balustrade ran along one side, underlining a view of the valley and the hazy blue mountains in the distance. By leaning over the rail, I could see my seventh-grade classmates playing their racing, skillful games in the school yard below. I longed to be with them, adding my voice to the laughter which occasionally found its way up the hill and danced in the air until the wind folded it down on itself, washed it away, and returned the hilltop to silence.

I perched on the railing, waiting for my breathing to come back to normal, knowing that when the Señora opened the heavy carved door and waved me in, I would need all the lung power I could summon. She left no holes in her conversation and tolerated none in mine.

A tall hatchety woman dressed always in black, the Señora had a voice abrasive and challenging and, in the evenings, when the crows flew above the town from tree to noisy tree, I often wondered if she might be one of them. The Señora's sight was failing and she needed someone to read the Bible to her in English. My parents decided this was a wonderful opportunity for me to learn about altruism, to earn a little spending money, and to be introduced to the world of classical literature, all at the same time. I hated the idea and begged for an alternative after-school activity — anything — piano lessons, weaving lessons, *ballet* lessons, but I respected my parents and feared Señora Corego so up I climbed.

I read to her for three long hours three afternoons a week. Near the end of the second week, as I rested on the railing, wondering if the hill was high enough and steep enough for a suicide leap, the Señora opened the door before I knocked.

"You're late, young man." She shut the door behind me and motioned me toward the polished wooden reading stand which held a black leather Bible, its gilt-edged pages always open. With a sigh, she lowered herself into her rocking chair and gazed out across the desert. "The second chapter of Deuteronomy," she said, "and I would appreciate it if you would try to stay awake!"

The Señora would correct my pronunciation and, now and then, ask me if I hadn't skipped over something — which I sometimes did because the warmth of the room and the uniform tone of my own voice put me to sleep. As I struggled for balance astride the wake-sleep barrier, words from the sleep side would occasionally infiltrate a Bible passage and the Señora would become angry.

This particular afternoon was unusually warm. I slid help-lessly down the slippery, somnolent slope and into a dream about baseball. Matthew, Mark, and Luke began shouting encouragement from the dugout. I was awakened by a louder shout from the Señora.

"What's the matter with you? Why didn't you sleep last night?!"

I was instantly awake and my answer popped out in one breath, unhampered by thought.

"Because a man came to our house," I said, "and pulled my Mom out of bed and up onto his big white horse and rode into the desert with her."

I had no idea where the fabrication had come from, but my drowsiness was gone.

The old woman turned her chair toward me, rocked it forward, and locked it in that position with her feet. Curiosity softened her voice.

"Your mother was taken away during the night? Did you call the police?"

"Oh no," I said. "He always brings her back."

"This has happened before? You know this man?"

"No, but Mom does, I guess." Señora Corego looked at me in silence, the fingers of one hand covering her mouth as if to keep it from dropping open. "I think the guy on the horse is one of the men who took off with my Dad."

"We haven't time for this," she said, wrinkling her eyes at an ornate clock on the wall and waving a hand in the air as if to dissipate the interruption like a bad smell.

The following session I was again dueling with the angel of sleep, holding firmly to the reading stand in case my knees should buckle in the heat of battle. I reached the end of Leviticus and glanced at the Señora, but I got the feeling she had stopped listening.

Unexpectedly, she said, "Your Dad. What did you mean, he *took off?*"

It took a moment of mental scrambling to recall what she was talking about. "Oh. Well. I guess he decided he wanted to be somewhere else."

"Where did he want to be?"

"I don't know. I think he saw a show on TV about Mexican cowboys. He bought a horse and a cowboy outfit and rode off into the desert with two guys he met in a bar. Three born-again gouchos, my Mom called them — their heads full of dreams, their saddle bags full of ice and Dos Equis beer."

The Señora held up her hand for me to stop. She nodded toward the Bible. "Enough. Where were we now?"

The next time I visited, King Solomon was the order of the day. I had been reading for about an hour and was doing a pretty good job of holding Morpheus at bay, when I looked over at the Señora. She had a dreamy look as if she were somewhere else, perhaps hearing the song of distant birds rather than the song of Solomon.

When I hesitated for a moment, she surprised me by asking, "Was you mother very sad when he was gone?"

"Only for a few hours," I said. "She met a guy named Paulo at the market and they got to talking about the meaning of life and that kind of stuff, and they decided to go to India together — that afternoon — to *jump-start their enlightenment* as Paulo put it.

"Oh no," the Señora said. "How awful for you."

"It was okay," I reassured her. "Paulo turned out to be a Mormon on a mission so she came home." The old woman touched my arm and seemed relieved.

Gradually I found I no longer dreaded my visits up the hill. Even the climb required less effort. Her voice had new life and my stories continued to pop out of nowhere, sometimes surprising us both and making us laugh.

I told her about my dad winning at Wimbledon four years in a row and she told me about her husband, a handsome Mexican business man who wore white linen suits and how she had met him when she was a young woman living in Boston. I told her about the time our family had been captured by hippies and forced to live on grits and granola for a year and she told me more about her husband — that he had died soon after they moved into this, their dream house. I told her about the time Mom fell out of an airplane and she told me that she had never bothered to learn Spanish because she had always expected that one day her husband would walk back in through the front door and they would once again communicate without words.

One warm afternoon in late summer, when I could hardly wait to tell her about the time my dog had died and been prayed back to life, the Señora held up her hand for me to stop.

"Enough. No stories today. What I need right now is the Book of Psalms. Please begin with the twenty third." Her voice sounded tired as if it had traveled a long way before reaching her lips. She moved more slowly than usual and the wrinkled skin of her neck seemed more pale, almost translucent.

While I wandered through the valley of the shadow of death, fearing no evil, the old woman stared out the window. I finished the last Psalm, but she said nothing so I wandered around in the

Book of Proverbs until it was time for me to leave. I said good-bye. She waved to me over her shoulder, but seemed distracted and held her gaze on the mountains to the East.

On my next visit, resting on the railing and rearranging some red flowers I had picked on my way up, I wondered what my next story would be. The Señora failed to open the door despite several *whaps* with the heavy iron knocker. I tried the door. It opened and I went in. The Señora was in her rocker looking out across the desert, out beyond her private, blurred space. Her face seemed less wrinkled, peaceful, and she was smiling. I touched her arm, but she didn't respond. I put my ear close to her face. She wasn't breathing.

I wasn't frightened, but silent loneliness began to fill the big room and I ran back down the hill.

September arrived and my parents' sabbatical was over. My Dad had finished his doctoral thesis on Formations of the Mexican Desert and it was time for our family to drive back home. As we headed north, I looked back through the swirling dust at the village and the big stucco house perched above it. We were a considerable distance out of town, but I thought I saw the heavy carved door standing open and a tall, dark haired man in a white linen suit standing just inside, bowing slightly and holding a bouquet of red flowers behind his back.

Slow Dance

The rain stops. The sky turns the puddles and gutters along Market Street into blue mirrors. Saturday afternoon, the sidewalks are deserted — one of those polished, blue and white days that occasionally sparkle through San Francisco in late winter. Tommy finishes his job and, whistling happily to himself, hustles his tools out the kitchen door of the restaurant. He swings his wooden tool box up and into the back of his pickup. On the door of the truck: Tommy Hendrickson, Cabinets & Fixtures, Lic. #38624, 383-1012.

Trees in the park across the street rattle in last night's leftover wind, their black trunks almost invisible in the deep shade. Torn blankets and plastic shower curtains are spread out to dry on a damp concrete wall. Tommy heads back into the building to grab his ladder. He wishes a good day to the young Latino cooks and bumps his ladder through the kitchen, out to his truck. He leans against a fender and shakes free of his coveralls, enjoying the retreat of the gray clouds like balls of unbleached cotton over the Oakland hills. He swings the ladder up and ties it down, giving the hitch a last tug and taking a final look into the bed of his truck — but the spot where he put his toolbox, the same place he always puts his tool box, is empty.

He darts a look at the wet pavement beside the truck in case he left the toolbox on the ground. Perspiring, he runs back into the building on the chance that the box was left inside — but he knows it wasn't. He rushes back out; the light is too bright, the view too clear. His beloved mahogany toolbox, his old friend that he had built while still an apprentice, has been stolen.

Shocked, dazed by how suddenly a glorious day can turn dark and cold, he looks up and down the street, runs up the block and checks around the corner of a building — nobody carrying a toolbox and no police around. His white pickup truck glistens in the sunshine.

The only activity Tommy can see is movement under the trees in the little park across the street. Perhaps someone under there may have seen what happened. He enters the park and looks around dimly while his eyes get used to the darkness. Oversized leaf-held raindrops splash his face and splat onto plastic tarps.

Benches line both sides of a meandering, paved pathway, all of them occupied. Tommy moves slowly past the closest encampment, peering at the chaos of human acquisitiveness; a white toaster with the fingers of three black gloves groping out of the slots, a bag of plastic bags, a Monopoly board folded inside out and faded.

The park smells of damp cardboard, over-ripe bananas, and urine. Tommy bends forward, peers under a ragged edge.

"What the hell you looking at?"

"I'm looking for my tools, wondering if anyone here might have seen someone take a box out of that white truck over there."

"Get your ass outta' here." The rasping voice of a woman.

Tommy continues up the line. A young man with matted hair sits on the wet ground, wrapped in Safeway bags.

Tommy moves on, ignoring mumbled curses, seeking someone

else to speak to. He wants to run, but where to? To shout, but at whom? He peers out into the sunshine, still no police.

A little farther up the path, in the middle of the walkway, two shopping carts have been lashed together with electrician's tape. Chrome is peeling off their rusted steel frames, their plastic handles faded and cracked. In spite of a missing wheel, the two carts are moving — very slowly. A tall, weathered man with a stained gray beard and dressed in stitched-together brown rags, the Jolly Green Giant with leaf blight, is walking backwards in slow, short steps, towing the little train with its mountain of possessions. Tommy catches up.

Suddenly he glimpses varnished wood, a familiar shape. The toolbox is right there — perched brazenly on one of the carts, not even covered. The man in rags watches Tommy and waits. Tommy takes two quick steps, reaches out for his toolbox.

"Give me that!" he says to the man. His hand touches the mahogany — but from the corner of his eye he catches a movement beside the cart and jumps back just as the teeth of a lunging, green-eyed dog snap together within inches of his chest. The dog is tethered to the cart by a length of black lamp-cord. Tommy glares at the dog, then at its owner.

"You crazy? That dog's gonna' hurt somebody!"

The rag man chuckles through missing teeth, his voice cold and rough like the wet pavement.

"Am I crazy? I'm not the one who almost got hisself bit." He takes another slow, backward step.

"Look, I don't have time for your bullshit word games. Just give me my tools and I won't say anything to anybody. We'll pretend it never happened."

"Hey, I got a better idea." The rag man isn't smiling anymore.

"Why don't *you* pretend it never happened and get your ass out'a here and *I* won't say anything to anybody."

"Okay, gimme my tools."

"You didn't hear what I said." The man takes another small step back, drawing the carts with him. Tommy steps forward; the dog growls. Tommy looks around, out to the bright, sunny sidewalk. No help in sight.

Their slow dance has aroused the bench dwellers; tarps crackle, blankets are being rolled up and tied.

The rag man looks at Tommy and smiles. Without warning, he reaches forward into the open toolbox, scoops out an electric drill, and, in one smooth swing, tosses it high over Tommy's shoulder. Tommy turns, runs after it a few steps, and watches as a dark figure reaches forward from his bench and catches the tool. As Tommy approaches, the figure stands up, big. Tommy turns back to the carts.

His block-plane flies over his head and is caught, then a measuring tape. A set of chisels flies free of its canvas roll, clatters to the pavement like a handful of dropped silverware, and disappears. Frantically, Tommy looks out from his nightmare, out into the sunshine. His white truck gleams in the sun.

The rag man continues to distribute the tools. Tommy watches helplessly: screw drivers, a steel square, a hammer, pliers, another screw driver — until the box is empty.

Tommy and the rag man reach the end of the park and move slowly through the lace-edged shadows, out into the sunlight. Their dance has carried them out onto a large black parking lot, almost empty, where the sun lifts steam out of the drying pavement. Tommy takes a moment to look around. A phone booth stands at the end of the block; he gauges the distance. If he moves fast enough, he can reach it, make a quick call, and still keep the caravan in sight. The rag man watches.

As Tommy turns to run, the rag man sets the empty toolbox down on the pavement and moves slowly away from it. The box is out of the dog's range now; Tommy hurries over and picks it up. Just as he starts to run, a patrol car rolls around the corner. He rushes over to it, waving the toolbox.

The driver slows to a stop, finishes a conversation with his partner, and eases the window open a crack. "What's the problem?"

Frantic, Tommy tells his story and points at the strange caravan in the parking lot.

The two officers are walking now, toward the carts — Tommy leads the way, the rag man waits, unmoving, unconcerned. He has placed a metal bowl on the ground and poured out some water for the dog which now lies quietly in the warm sunshine.

"You got a license for that dog?"

"Sure do, officer. Right here, current too." He pulls two metal tags out of a plastic bag and holds them up. Tommy waits, the empty tool box hanging at his side.

Again the policeman speaks to the rag man. "This gentleman says you have his tools."

The rag man smiles. "I don't have his tools. You're welcome to look." He holds his arms out over the carts, palms up.

"No, no!" Tommy shouts. "Those people over *there* have my tools." He indicates the direction with a nod over his shoulder, but when he turns to look, the park is empty.

Art Works

Venice Beach mourns lost graffiti. Cleanup crew goofed,
painted over 20 years worth of popular street art.

—San Francisco Chronicle

Paolo and I paint houses for Purvis Painting and Decorating.
Mr. Purvis has been painting and decorating this arty little
beach town for over thirty years. He hires the locals, mostly
artists, because they are good with their hands and good with
color, but mostly he hires us because we work for short money.
Our art feeds our souls and Purvis Painting and Decorating takes
care of everything else — food, shelter, and art supplies.

Paolo and I are both painters. Some people call us vandals,
defacers, worse than that, but we're graffiti artists.

Last year Paolo came out here from The Bronx without
much more than an old brown guitar case and an attitude
about art. In New York, he told me, you work as fast as you can,
then run like hell. Paolo got tired of running. When he read
about "The Pit" here in Venice Beach, a place where spray-can
Cezannes work on sun-washed walls in broad daylight, their
work respected, he knew it was time to make a move.

We went out painting together as soon as he arrived. Right
away I could see he was really good. His straight lines were like
lasers, his curves like rainbows, and his colors, his colors blended
as naturally as the wet, damp, and dry sand on the beach. The

passion in his work grabbed me somewhere inside my chest and I wanted only to work with Paolo for the rest of my life—the Rodgers and Hart of aerosol artistry, and that ratty old guitar case he carries around all the time: twenty three built-in compartments, spray cans, twenty three different colors.

The Pit that drew Paolo out here is a seating area at the back of the beach about the size of an amoebae-shaped basketball court. It has tables and benches made of concrete and a gently curving wall to keep out the ocean winds. It is the inside surface of this wall that became famous for its graffiti.

About two weeks ago, Mr. Purvis phoned about some more work. Early the next morning, in a chilling fog that swirled when we walked and wet our clothes, five artists, Paolo and myself among them, waited uncomfortably in The Pit—three graffiti artists, a portrait painter, and one hungry-looking saxophone player. Mr. Purvis arrived and stood on a bench, pleased with the piece of official-looking paper he was holding up for us to see—pale yellow with black print and red highlighting.

"A contract from the city," he announced. "A contract to paint The Pit." He waved the paper back and forth in front of us. "Two coats on everything; tables, benches, and both sides of the wall."

It sounded to me like a nice job, about three day's work ... until the last part sunk in.

"What did you say about the wall?" someone asked.

"Two coats inside and out," Purvis repeated.

Silence and disbelief swirled with the fog.

"The inside of the wall?"

"Look, it's not my idea. Two new guys on the city council came up with it."

We stood dazed, searching each other's faces, a joke, right?

"This is bullshit!" The saxophone player pulled his wool hat down over his ears and headed for an exit. My mind was a blur, as if the fog had gotten inside. The portrait painter drifted away without a word. Mr. Purvis waited.

"Anybody?" Silence.

Then, suddenly, a voice, "Hell, I'll do it. I'll get a crew together and just do it."

It was Paolo speaking! Paolo the artist!

I felt confused, then angry, then just very cold. I walked home alone.

～

When the CAUTION—KEEP OUT signs came down and the public saw what had happened to The Pit, the reaction was swifter and louder than anyone could have imagined. Television programs, newspaper articles, and phone calls—thousands of phone calls pounded city hall, buried the Chamber of Commerce, and frightened the mayor. A generic press release went out; *an unfortunate mistake blah blah, a breakdown in communications blah blah, a regrettable error that will be thoroughly investigated blah blah blah.*

Meanwhile, I didn't see much of Paolo, didn't want to. But then, yesterday, Paolo sent out word that he wanted to see all the graffiti artists the next morning in The Pit. Nine o'clock. Apology time, I figured. I didn't feel like going, but I went. I guess I still like the guy even if he did do something really stupid.

The inside of The Pit had the ugly emptiness of a vacant
house with no curtains on the windows. At nine, Paolo arrived.
He sat down on one of the tables with his feet on a bench and
we all settled onto benches nearby.

Look," he said. "I know you guys are pissed at me, but let
me tell you how I feel about this whole thing, okay? I came to
Venice to do art. But art is what happens to you, what goes
on inside you while you're working at it. It isn't what you end
up with. So that's why I painted the wall." He looked around.
Without waiting for an answer he went on. "And here's what's
happening now. Yesterday I went to a city council meeting.
Those guys are all pissed at each other and none of them know
how to turn down the heat. So I gave them a suggestion. I told
them we would replace the art work."

"That's crazy! You mean you told them we'd replace it, the
stuff that was there?" someone asked.

"No. You know art doesn't work that way! I told them we'd
replace it—better than before."

"And they went for it?"

"Jumped at it. Of course we had a few things to straighten
out, like they wanted it completed by next weekend, but I told
them art doesn't work that way either. I told them it would be
an on-going, organic type thing that would continue to unfold
and surprise them, possibly for years."

"They still went for it?"

"They grumped a little, but they have no choice." Paolo
reached into his pocket and pulled out a piece of paper; yellow
with red highlighting.

"You got us a contract to do graffiti?"

"Right here." He waved the paper over his head as if to dry

the ink. Then he smiled. "And they offered to pay us a dollar an hour—but I told them no, art doesn't work that way either. I said we would need at least five bucks an hour, six if we work on weekends with the tourists watching."

I was surprised. I didn't know art could be worked that way.

Bus to Madness

Tag Malone, the first passenger to arrive, boards the waiting commuter van and scowls at Zoomer, the driver. Zoomer has the morning paper spread across the steering wheel and doesn't notice. Tag isn't sure he can stand another morning commute: the sameness, the gray dullness, the screaming boredom. He takes a seat on the right side of the bus, the shady side, leaving his mirrored sunglasses on for privacy. The right side of the bus will be the shady side all the way down to the city. Tag likes it that way. He feels safer on the shady side, no prying sunshine spotlighting him for the world to inspect. Tag never inspects himself, why should other people get a clear shot at him?

Tag hates this commute, leaving at the same time every day, taking the same route with the same strange people — major boring. If he were to squeeze all his boredom together into one big buoyant lump, he knows it would lift him right out the window and up into the cool morning sky. But then he wouldn't get to his job at the Digi-Zap Corporation, creators of the world's most violent video games.

A mayhem maven, Tag's job at Digi-Zap is to name and decide how to kill the dodging, slashing warriors that chase each other around the screen; Bloody Billy, Mike The Strike, Mick deMaim, those are all Tag's inventions. Digi-Zap gave him a ten thousand dollar bonus for Mick deMaim and three thousand in stock options for Pop Chop and Fred Dead.

The second passenger to climb aboard the bus is Shotgun Yap, leader of the Zoomer Support Group and Fan Club. Shotgun, as usual, sits in the front seat next to Zoomer, his hero. He launches his usual non-stop, co-pilot spiel into Zoomer's right ear, praising his driving ability and directing a steady stream of curses at any vehicle coming within ten feet of the bus — and the engine isn't even running yet.

Tiltin' Milton enters next, his over-stuffed briefcase pulling down his shoulder, giving him a permanent starboard list. Milton looks around at the empty seats, then sits where he always sits, behind Zoomer. All the passengers sit in the same seat every day, a carry-over, Tag figures, from the first grade where teachers assigned seats and yelled at you if you moved.

Milton begins speaking into Zoomer's left ear while Shotgun fills in from the right. The two men laugh appreciatively at everything Zoomer says and, like a bartender or a rock star, Zoomer expects it.

The next passenger to come through the door is Benny the Bomber, a short, dark-bearded man with a protruding round stomach, smudged glasses and a permanently knitted brow. Bomber ignores Zoomer and the flight crew and glares his way down the aisle clutching his black, metal lunch box, speaking to no one, frowning at the floor. He leans forward when he walks, as if he always wishes he were a little ahead of where he actually is. Bomber sits down, holds the black box up to his ear, and gives it a little shake before setting it down with great care. So it won't go off, Tag figures.

Tag watches Rugsy come in next. Rugsy wears an unconvincing toupee swept low above one eye. He is a tall, sad-faced man in his mid thirties, a salesman, Tag figures, who hands out smiles to his customers all day and can't afford to waste any on his way to work. Rugsy looks around expectantly as if he might find all new people, and then assumes his normal, disappointed visage. His deep-set eyes and projecting chin fold together easily into a grump and seem comfortable that way.

Tag shrinks down in his seat as Penelope Danish steps aboard. Unlike The Bomber and Rugsy, she will talk to any-body about anything and will stray from her assigned seat to do it. So much conversation bubbles out of her, that Tag always carries an open book on his lap. If she slides in next to him, offers him a goodie from her wrinkled bakery bag, and jumps into her story about her poodle, her husband, and the stress of having to choose between them, Tag becomes absorbed in his book and she moves on.

When Polly and Molly flutter in through the doorway, Tag sits up with a start. The two women dress like macaws, and chatter like canaries. They smile at Tag and take seats opposite him where they flutter their skirts into place and preen their hair smooth in the sunshine.

Tag wonders about the Queen. Zoomer has now started the engine but the Queen has not yet arrived. Maybe this is one of her especially regal days, Tag figures. Perhaps she is lingering late over crumpets. The queen is an attractive young woman who wears high black boots and carries an immaculate Burberry folded on her arm. Tag once attempted conversation with the Queen, but she was more interested in checking her curls in her silver mirror than conversing with a commoner. She may have a lot on her schedule today, Tag decides — hours and hours of commanding and decreeing, perhaps a beheading. The chauf-feur will be bringing her into town in the Bentley.

The bus pulls out into traffic and begins its non-stop run into the city. Zoomer zooms, Shotgun watches in every direction, and Milton checks the progress of the trip, delivering a running commentary into Zoomer's left ear as if he were broadcasting a soccer game.

Tag stares out the window, same route. He looks at his fellow passengers, same weird people. He listens to the flight crew, same mixture of encouragement for Zoomer and derision for everybody else on the road. Tag is not sure he can endure the boredom that is freezing his liver and turning his eyes inside out. He presses his knees hard against the seat in front of him but the bus doesn't go any faster.

Then something wonderful happens. As they enter the city, a heavy red truck charges in from the right. Despite shouts and curses from the flight crew, there is a crash and the bus rolls over onto its left side, a slow roll — a lot of surprise, broken glass, and minor spurts of blood, but nothing serious. Zoomer, dazed and well bruised, struggles to reach a little metal crank handle that used to be over the windshield, but is now next to it. With painful effort, he turns the handle until the sign on the front of the bus reads Out of Service. Everyone applauds. Polly and Molly have fallen across the aisle and landed on top of Tag. As they struggle to stand up, their spike heels tear Tag's shirt and poke painfully into his back. He groans a little, and when they realize that the softness under foot is Tag, they step off.

With the bus lying on its side, the left side windows show close-ups of black asphalt, the right side windows have become skylights, and the entry door a hatch. Tag struggles to his feet and looks around. His sunglasses have been knocked off and his back hurts. He climbs up and out the open door. "All *right!*" he shouts pumping his right arm. "That's more like it!" He jumps down and sprints the rest of the way to Digi-Zap, wondering what else he can look forward to this morning.

The Fence

A brown dog lives next door to us behind a harsh wooden fence—a strong dog of many kinds mixed together. He is not handsome, his head is too large for the rest of his body, but he is very smart.

The brown dog doesn't spend much time in his yard. He doesn't like to be trapped there and escapes every morning as soon as Mr. Paxton puts him out the back door and drives to work. Mr. Paxton has nailed scraps of wood all over the fence in every direction and all along the top. There are no gaps, but still the dog escapes.

A rough black tree stands in Mr. Paxton's yard near the fence and the dog is a scrambler. Every morning I hear him clawing and scraping the coarse bark — and then his frantic white-showing eyes rise into view. He elbows himself up and over the top board and launches himself, head first, into the ivy on our side of the fence. Then he shakes himself, shakes off the desperate residue of confinement, gives me a conspiratorial look, and bounces out of our yard to spend the rest of the day waiting for Mr. Paxton to come home. Late in the afternoon Mr. Paxton arrives and swears at the dog and nails more wood onto the fence. He tries hard to find out how his dog is escaping, afraid he will return one day and find the dog in the street, flat as a brown blanket.

Sometimes, in the morning, Mr. Paxton drives down the block and around the corner and then sneaks back to his house and watches the dog from his kitchen window. But the brown dog lies quietly in the sun and pretends to be asleep until Mr. Paxton is late for work. The moment Mr. Paxton leaves, the dog is over and out.

Occasionally, Mr. Paxton speaks to me through the fence, but we don't talk much. My wife always calls my name as soon as she hears me talking to him. She needs me to do some chore or another. She doesn't like all the swear words he uses. I told her that I'm too old to pick up any new bad habits, but she still calls my name right away and wants to know what we were talking about.

The other day, Mr. Paxton called to me through the fence. He asked me if I had any idea how the hell his goddamned dog kept getting out.

I stood up close and spoke directly to the rough, grey boards, right there where his voice was punching through like the points of his frantically driven nails. I had thought a lot about this matter, and was ready with the answer. I didn't tell him about the tree. I told him, "Mr. Paxton, your dog does not *believe* he can be imprisoned and, therefore, he can't."

Then my wife called my name. When I came into the house, she wanted to know what I had been talking to Mr. Paxton about.

I told her we had been discussing the indomitable nature of freedom.

She told me the kitchen garbage needed emptying.

Cool Smoke

Three years ago I kicked the nicotine habit, kicked it for a girl who later moved to Cleveland and left me with nothing but clean ashtrays and an overbearing sense of self-righteousness.

From the window of my second floor office, I enjoy looking down, literally and figuratively, on the smokers from our building. They stand outside in little puffing groups, the cast of characters changing according to the hour.

Early last month, mid-morning, I happened to look down and immediately noticed something different about the way the ten o'clock group was acting — something strange, a new energy. The men were over-laughing and striking intricate poses of exaggerated relaxation. Then I saw why. A woman, new to the group and drop-dead beautiful, had them acting like grease ants around a cookie crumb.

When she reappeared the next day I was already at my window. I saw only her. I watched the way she smiled, accepted a light, laughed, the way the wind blew her hair and the way she brushed it off her face and turned to go back to work. Each detail touched my soul like a light spring rain that you feel on your face or the back of your hand before it makes anything wet. She soaked into me and I had to meet her.

This, however, as any man will tell you, is not simple with such a woman. You have to be *cool*. When the time is right, you have to let the conversation evolve naturally out of some shared observation, something subtle, sensitive. This isn't high school where you wait by her locker and ask her about the math assignment. This is the majors!

The building where I work has five street entrances, twelve elevators, fifteen different companies. Trusting *kismet* just does not work. There was only one place where I knew I could find her; with the ten o'clock smoking group, and that's where I would have to be. Of course I couldn't just stand among the smokers, arms dangling from my shoulders, and start a conversation. What would I do with my hands? Without a cigarette, I would stand out like a worm in a tank of eels, not cool at all.

When ten o'clock arrived I rode the elevator down, popped a handful of coins into the cigarette machine, and *thunk, clunk, whap*, a pack of Lucky Strikes landed in the chrome tray. I stepped outside and there she was, sweeter than life and holding a pack of Pall Malls. I made a mental note to switch brands and I lit my first cigarette in three years. A grabbing cough threatened to blow my cover but I stuffed it and stayed cool.

I was enjoying the smoke so much that I lost concentration and she headed back into the building before I could even think of an opener. I went back to my office feeling empty.

When I came out the next day, she was already in earnest conversation with a tall redheaded guy whom I recognized from our sales department. I leaned nonchalantly against a granite column and took deep pulls, close enough to hear the ragged edges of their conversation but far enough to be *cool*. He looked over and raised an eyebrow, a greeting, but not one that would allow me to insinuate myself into their conversation. After that, the window of opportunity remained locked. I watched them leave, had another cigarette, and went back to work.

The next day I came down for my smoke a little before ten but neither of them showed up. By ten thirty I had finished three Pall Mall's and my head had begun to ache.

I went back to my office. Clearly it was time to compromise my *subtlety* standards. *Cool* would have to slip a little. I picked up the first two pieces of paper that came to hand, dropped them into a manila folder, and tucked it under my arm. I took the elevator up to sales.

Our sales department consists of six guys at lined-up desks, each tilting his head to hold a telephone, each speaking as if he had his best friend on the line. I spotted my red-haired co-smoker right away and wandered toward his desk without apparent purpose, as if I were surfacing in a swimming pool and looking around to get my bearings. He hung up the phone and smiled. "Hi, what can I do for ya'?"

"Oh, hi ... uh ... nothing really. Just came up to check a few figures. How you doin'?"

"Doin' great."

"I didn't see you and your friend at smoke break this morning. Uh ... What's her name again?" I frowned in concentration to indicate it was right on the tip of my tongue, that I really knew her.

"Marcie."

"Oh yeah, Marcie. She's great, isn't she? She still with the same company?"

"I guess so. We've never talked about that."

"She must be on vacation, uh? She's usually pretty consistent with that smoke break."

"No, I don't think she's on vacation. I went to a meeting

with her just last night. She didn't mention vacation."

My heart dropped. They were tighter than I thought.

"A meeting? Uh ... One of those after-hours business-net-working things?"

"No, this is more important than that. This can change your whole life; your health, your outlook, everything."

"Sounds like EST," I said, surprised at how sour it came out.

"Better than that! I haven't had a smoke in three days. I'm going to kick it this time, so's Marcy. It's called Smoke-Enders. It'll turn your whole life around. You oughta' give it a try."

I thanked him and rode the elevator down to the lobby. He was right, of course. I could see a pattern emerging. I stepped outside and lit a cigarette. As the smoke swirled around my head, the solution became clear. Time to give up women.

Done

Tracy and I were living in Manhattan and publishing a magazine that we had started when we were journalism students at Cornell. The magazine took up most of our time, its detritus, most of our apartment. The name of the magazine was DONE — *a compendium of everything being done anywhere by anybody.* We wrote the entire magazine ourselves and tried not to miss anything.

Perhaps it was this overly-ambitious focus which caused the undoing of DONE, but three o'clock one morning, while we were sitting across from each other at the kitchen table, crunching biscotti crumbs into the blue Formica with a jug of Merlot, we realized DONE was finished, our word-child had gotten away from us, lost direction.

David Blast, a critic writing in the New York Guardian, had referred to our magazine as "... a purveyor of drive-by hipness and celebrity hype, catering to semi-educated, computerized children of all ages."

That review was part of the reason we decided to redirect the magazine, to transform DONE into a gentle anthology of poetry and short prose, to aim it at "anybody with a quality soul" as Tracy put it.

We named our new publication SOULARITY and placed a small ad in a writer's magazine soliciting submissions. We failed to realize, however, that in this country there are more writers than rain drops. Manuscripts instantly filled our lives, inundating our apartment, a rising paper tide. We side-stepped carefully among the towering stacks, in danger of being buried under cascading creativity. Every day we shoveled ourselves a little clearing and sat and read — just read and read. We read more hours than a man should be awake.

In order to keep our heads above the postman's daily deluge, we found it necessary to adjust our editorial criteria. Desperate, we began rejecting manuscripts for such shortcomings as careless stamp-clustering on the envelope, return addresses from unhip parts of the country, or any other capricious and arbitrary reason that looked like a buoyant straw to our drowning, word-soaked minds.

DONE no longer shared space with ME, US, and PEOPLE on the impulse racks at grocery store check stands. Instead, SOULARITY shared bookstore and coffee house space with literary journals bearing arcane and presumably intellectual names like ZYZZYVA, CONVOLVULUS, and LYNX EYE. We sold an occasional copy every other month; our finances got tight.

One evening, as we cleaned our eye glasses and refilled our coffee cups for the twelfth time since lunch, Tracy said, "If we had a dollar for every manuscript we've read, we'd be rich as Donald Trump."

"Well, why not," I said, sitting down on the floor of my little clearing, taking her by the hand, and pulling her down beside me. "That's a hell of an idea! Suppose we charged a *reading fee* for each submission? These people are crazy to see their stuff in print."

"A dollar a story," she said.

"Two dollars for poems," I suggested. "Poems never make sense the first time through."

"Instead of a *reading fee*," she said, "let's call it a *submission fee*. That way we can read as many or as few as we choose and publish whatever we wish — and to save time, we'll assure them that MANUSCRIPTS WILL NOT BE RETURNED. This is the computer age. They can always print themselves another copy."

"That's great," I said. "It sends the message that they wouldn't want it back anyway, dog-eared as it must be after our extensive stable of editors has gone over it again and again." Tracy and I hugged each other, put away our reading glasses, and went to bed.

That brainstorming session brought our fiscal fumbling to an end. *Submission fees* rolled in and *reading fees* also found their place. *Reading fees*, we discovered, could be as high as twenty dollars, as long as the piece was labeled ENTRY and sent to one of our frequent Short Story Contests or Poetry Competitions. In short, we had learned the ins and outs of the publishing business.

~

Tracy and I have now retired, a career move made possible by an invention of ours called THE CLUTTER CUTTER — an automated conveyor which runs directly from mail slot to money extractor to debris box.

We've done very well. Every publisher in the country now uses one of our machines.

Work Clothes

The sign on the 57th Street entrance said: EMPLOYEES ONLY. Frank Delaney hurried in, slamming the heavy door behind him. The room was damp and hot, the old building's heating system over-compensating for the icy storm blowing outside.

A line of dusty light bulbs hung from the ceiling and spread a begrudging orange glow over the lockers that lined two walls. Frank walked over and lowered himself onto one of the wooden benches which ran down the center of the room, mounted on rusted steel pipes, bolted down. A prison, he thought, an absolute fucking prison. Little pools of dirty water formed on the concrete floor as the frozen slush on his boots began to melt. He stared across the room at nothing in particular, putting off for as long as possible the putting on of his work clothes.

Solly Rosen, who had worked the previous shift, hung his uniform in a locker across the room and began getting into his street clothes. Frank looked over at him and caught his eye.

"How'd it go?"

"Same old stuff. Everybody wants something different." Solly buttoned his shirt.

Frank unwrapped his scarf and shook his shoulders free of his heavy wool coat. "Boy, I know what you mean. Everybody wants something different. And my wife's the worst of the bunch of them." He waited but Solly didn't respond. "Every penny I make here, she needs for clothes for those goddamned kids of hers."

"You divorced?" Solly asked.

"No, we're together. But she spoils the shit out of 'em. Anything they want, she buys — new clothes, fancy basketball shoes, any damn thing they can think of. If it was up to me, their clothes would come from St. Vincent's like mine did, and if they whined about it, I'd whack 'em across the head."

Solly stopped buttoning his overcoat and came over to where Frank was angrily jerking his work clothes out of the rattling steel locker.

"You like kids?" Solly asked him.

"Kids?" He stared at Solly as if it were a trick question. "No, not much. As far as I'm concerned they're all a bunch of lazy bastards who live in front of tv sets and complain when you ask them to move over. They don't know what the hell it means to earn a livin'. Two jobs I'm workin' right now!" Frank looked closely at Solly. "Why you askin' me that?"

"Just wondering." Solly finished buttoning his coat. He extended his hand. "Today was my last shift. Maybe I'll see you again some time."

Frank watched Solly leave. He struggled into his work clothes, stopped at a mirror where he stroked his beard for a moment, then opened a door and stepped out into a large, bright room.

Kids and their parents waited in an impatient line that squaggled this way and that through the toy department.

"Well, well," he said. "Merry Cristmas everybody."

"MERRY CHRISTMAS, SANTA!" came the response of delighted young voices.

Juxtaposing in Winston

Mike Blair whistled to himself as he headed into downtown Winston for something to eat. His purple silk bowling shirt was fresh from the cleaners and his new jeans felt just the right tightness for long strides in the cool night air.

The town of Winston had recently been discovered by the heavy earners of Silicon Valley, bringing many dollars — and considerable change. Houses the size of high-schools popped out of the hillsides; every gleaming car carried an abrasive, neck-snapping horn to announce green lights and punish hesitant drivers. Personal trainers arrived, experts on diet, perspiration, and the Zen of exercycle maintenance.

Mike, a Winston native, had been a furniture mover, but after subscribing to Muscle Magazine and buying some black tank-tops, he turned into a personal trainer. He stepped out briskly, hungry after a tiring day watching his clients lift, squeeze, push, climb, pull, peddle, and row themselves into shape.

He crossed Third Street and stopped in front of a store window so brightly lit that the sidewalk glowed with the blue-white intensity of a welder's arc. Blinking at the brightness, Mike looked inside. He blinked again. A horse's head, mounted like a hunting trophy and illuminated by spotlights, looked down from a tall white wall. A narrow fish drooped down from both sides of the horse's mouth like a handle-bar mustache.

The room was filled with well-dressed people standing around in small groups, holding drinks and talking. A woman stood with two young men in serious conversation while looking up at the horse and the fish.

Above the front window, a blue and white sign in stylish, hard-to-read neon said: THE SHELLEY HUDSON GALLERY. A glass door stood open to the right and Mike walked over for a better look. A young woman beckoned to him.

"Hello, come on in," she said, leaning forward, offering both hands, shuddering with warmth. "I'm Shelley Hudson. So glad you were able to make it."

"Oh, it was easy," Mike said. "The door was open and I just live around the corner." She smiled, held onto his hand, and drew him inside, firmly, as if he had been expected. Shelley guided him over to the white wall and, once again, looked up at the horse. Mike spotted a small card at eye level: #1 HORSE WITH FISH — $80,000.

"Isn't the horse wonderful?" she said. "To me, this piece says it all, the *mission statement* of the show if you know what I mean . . . don't you think? Did you come all the way down just for my opening?"

"Down?"

"From New York? From San Francisco? All these people came down for the opening of my show. Absolutely everybody's here." She swung her arm, palm up, to indicate "everybody."

"To tell you the truth," Mike said, "what I came down for was a ham and cheese on rye. What happened to Jerry's Deli that was here?"

"Oh, that little man's been gone for ages. We bought the building. Isn't it exciting?" She hooked a hand around Mike's

arm and pointed into the crowd. "That man over there in the
teal shirt with the mauve tie, that's Charles Whitman. He's the
editor of "The Art Street Journal." He's going to write a piece
about my show. Isn't that wonderful?"

"I guess," Mike said. "Hope he likes it."

"Oh, he loves it. He thinks we're just so brave, opening a
gallery way out here in the woods like this."

Mike had never thought of Winston, twenty minutes from San
Jose, as *out in the woods*. He looked around for familiar faces but
there weren't any. Shelley steered him toward a white-draped table
where trays of meticulously arranged canapés looked like exotic
board games and a man in a tuxedo was pouring drinks. "See?" she
said, "we even have ham sandwiches." They were about the size of
dominos. She took one, handed one to Mike, and ordered two
drinks. She called across the room to a short bald man in a ruffled
pink shirt and Reeboks. "Hello, sweetheart. So glad you could
make it." The man smiled, did a little dance, and waved back.

"Let me show you my pieces," she said. "I guess you've
already seen the horse.")

"First thing I noticed."

"Oh, good, then you like conceptual art."

"Well," he said, "I don't know much about it, but I know
what confuses me. What's the story on the fish?"

"Juxtaposition," she said. "The show's all about
Juxtaposition."

Mike nodded. Shelley led him over to a handsome mahogany table, beautifully carved and highly polished. A ten
foot Saguaro cactus appeared to have grown up through the
center of it, splintering the wood and peeling back the finish.
A hummingbird feeder, red and yellow plastic, hung from one

spiny arm. "Don't you just love it?" she said.

Mike looked at it for a while. A white tag on the table said: #4 MESA WITH PLANT — $33,000.

"Where'd you find the table?" he asked.

"Oh, I didn't find it. My people found it. I don't run around looking for things. I'm the artist. My part is the vision, the concept. That's why it's called conceptual art. I tell my crew what I need and they get it."

"And you assemble these things."

"No, silly. I'm an artist. My technicians assemble the exhibits."

"So you don't actually create anything."

"Well, certainly I do," she said. Her eyes darkened a little, but her happy face held. "I created this whole place. If it weren't for me, we'd be standing in a delicatessen right now." *And I wouldn't be so hungry*, Mike said to himself.

"Then you don't actually *build* anything."

"That's not my part of it. My job is to listen, to wait for the inspiration and breath it in, in-spiration, to accept whatever is given to me."

"Really. Sounds like a hell of a way to make a living," he said, "sort of a Buddhist thing, taking what's given to you and breathing." Shelley looked confused; Mike looked at the broken table. "Do you sell a lot of these things?"

"That's not the point," she said. "C'mon." She took his arm and walked him over to a glass tank as big as a Volkswagen. The tank contained an iMac computer and a metallic cross and was filled to the top with water.

"Hmm," he said. Mike knew she expected more, but he couldn't think of anything bright to say about a ruined computer and a rusting crucifix. Her smile wiggled a little, but managed to snap itself back into shape. A card taped to the glass said: #7 HOLY MAC-EREL — $60,000. Mike agreed — sixty thousand dollars, holy mackerel. "These things move pretty well?" he asked. "How many do you sell in a year?"

"None," she said. "I told you, that's not the point."

"Oh, okay. Then what's the point of the price tags?"

"The price tags contribute to the art."

"Those are pretty good sized contributions," he said.

"I'm not talking about money, I'm talking about contributing to the *impact* of the piece."

"The impact."

"Yes," she said, her voice slightly louder. "The whole idea is to make people feel something. The price tag contributes to that. Didn't you feel differently after you read the price tags?"

"Definitely. Mostly anger."

"See? then the price tags are contributing," she said. She looked up at Mike. "Why are you so interested in the prices? You're much too involved with money, you know that?"

"And you're not?"

"Not really. Like I said, I'm an artist. I take what's given to me."

"You're talking about inspiration again."

"Yes, but also I'm talking about my father. He helps me with the shows."

"Oh, he's the one who builds the exhibits while you're breathing in?"

"No. He's the one who buys the building and has it remodeled. After my show closes, the money we make from the franchise will pay for my next show. There are Shelley Hudson

Galleries in nine states."

A Safeway cart with black Porsche driving gloves draped over the handle held a mink jacket folded in its basket. A ten-foot fiberglass rabbit with long pierced ears sat in one corner wearing diamond earrings, twenty seven pairs. Nearby, several people stood around an open Bible suspended from the ceiling. A garden rake had been driven through the book, its handle penetrating the drywall behind the exhibit. The rake's curved tines emerged from between the pages and pointed heavenward. The tag said: #9 RAKING IT IN — $46,000. The man in the teal shirt was frowning at a pretty young woman with black lipstick and purple eyelashes who was arguing with him. Shelley went to get some more of those "precious little ham thingies" and Mike moved closer to the discussion.

"Well," the girl said in the knowing, confident voice of an art student, "I totally don't agree with you. If this is supposed to represent *all* mankind's heavenly yearnings, there would have to be like *thousands* of rakes, a whole gallery full of rakes, millions of 'em."

"You must understand," said the teal shirt, as if he were explaining the advantages of a potty to a two-year-old. "The artist doesn't try to reproduce life, he strives to clarify, to distill, if you will, a small portion of existence with which to communicate his vision to his fellow men."

"And women," the student corrected.

The man went on. "Art isn't truth, art is a lie that makes people see the truth."

"And what does *that* mean?" she asked.

"It's something Pablo Picasso said."

"That figures," said the lipstick. "His paintings don't make sense either." A few people laughed. Both communicants were playing to the crowd now and enjoying themselves immensely. "And why the King James Bible?" the girl wanted to know. "Why not the Koran or the Torah or the Talmud?"

Shelley returned, cradling two tiny sandwiches in a napkin.

"There seems to be a question about this piece," Mike told her. "The girl in the lipstick has a problem with it and the guy in the pink tie has a problem with her."

"Mauve," Shelley corrected.

"Well, maybe you should straighten them out," Mike said.

"Straighten them out? Oh no." She took his arm and skirted the crowd, turning her face away to avoid being recognized. "The important thing about art," she said, when they were clear of the group, "is that everyone sees each piece differently. If my art causes discussion, even arguments, then it's doing what it's supposed to do."

They approached a bright green John Deere tractor. Two pizza pies, eight feet across, had been baked, laminated in plastic, and bolted in place of the drive wheels. The card said: #12 TWO VEGETARIAN — EXTRA LARGE — $90,000.

"Is this one doing what it's supposed to do?" he asked.

"Isn't it perfect?" she said. "It just says it all, if you know what I mean?"

Mike's hunger was bearing down on his attitude. "I have no idea what you mean," he said. "I thought it was the horse by the front window that said it all."

"Oh . . . well it does, but this says all the rest, don't you think?"

"I'm sorry, Shelley, but I don't know what to think. I haven't any idea what these things are saying."

"Juxtaposition," she said. "Juxtaposition," a little louder the second time. Her smile cooled, changed shape several times like a just-blown soap bubble, and then she wasn't smiling at all. "The show directory is posted in the front window," she said. "Didn't you even bother to read it? Didn't you read what I wrote about the dynamic of unrelated entities and how their juxtaposition creates a dimension of total unity, shaping their inherent natures and without any communication whatsoever?"

"Guess I missed that," Mike said.

"Why do you think I coaxed you in off the street?" she said. As soon as I saw you I knew that you and I, together, would be the defining exhibit of my entire presentation." Her smile resurfaced. "Isn't it exciting? The juxtaposition of our entities has created an inherent dynamic that says it all without any communication whatsoever."

"That's pretty much the way I see it too," he said. He left through the glass door, out into the fresh night air to continue his search for a ham on rye juxtaposed with cheese: $3.75.

Henry's Wonder Leap

Henry Mack wonders if he really has to do this. He looks
down, down. He can smell the city traffic oozing, stop-
ping, and turning, on the black pavement thirty-three floors
below. A gray pigeon flies from one granite ledge to another and
preens its iridescent green neck. Henry leans out and feels his
center-of-gravity swing forward, like a slicing steel pendulum
compressing his panic, forcing it up between his shoulders. A
light wind moves his hair.

Just before his feet leave the railing, Henry notices a dime-
sized drop of blue paint near the big toe of his left shoe. He
remembers that drop of paint. Last weekend, while he helped
Carl and Dotty reflavor their living room, the spot on the shoe
had dried quickly and wouldn't rub off.

He bends his legs and leaps — out, out, onto the unsupportive
nothing.

Pretty Dotty, Henry thinks. If it weren't for her, I wonder if
any of this would be happening.

Henry recalls that acceleration is thirty-two feet per second
per second and wonders when terminal velocity will kick in.
And he wonders about that Einstein stuff, time changing shape
as things go faster and faster, or is it things change shape as time
goes faster and faster? Something like that. Wouldn't it be a
cruel trick, Henry wonders, if, when you are actually falling,
time were to slow down — and then stop — leaving you with

eternity to wonder what your son thinks of you, and whether or not you should have brought the dog along or left him with Margaret, your ex wife, who is going to call you selfish whether you take the dog along or not?

And Dotty, Henry wonders, isn't Dotty partially responsible? True, I was the one who brought over the marijuana, and I guess I knew what might happen, what I wanted to happen, but didn't Dotty know that Carl might come home early—like he did—and come into the house quickly —like he did—and catch us sweaty and not looking at each other and panic jamming into our clothes?

Could there be anything worse, Henry wonders, than getting caught in your son's, bedroom rushing your shorts on backwards after almost screwing his wife?

And poor old Spider, that smelly gray dog that can't run anymore. Henry wonders why Margaret never did like that dog. Even when he and Margaret were still married, she called the dog "that skinny animal." Guess she never understood that Spider is so much more than a dog, that he's a Whippet.

Henry wonders about a horrific stench that blows into his face. He looks down at the dog, which he is clutching to his chest like a parachute pack, and realizes that fear has opened Spider's anal gland. Henry opens his arms, but he and Spider stay together.

Henry wonders whether Spider ever thinks about death, whether he wonders about things the way Henry does, whether he understands that soon he will no longer be. Do dogs invent, the way humans do, and if so, what breed of dog is God?

And suddenly, neither of them wonders anymore.

Verbing

Mr. Fenton, an English teacher, decided he was right. Humanity really *was* moving faster and faster, its engine screaming, about to throw a rod. There, on the hardware store shelf, he had just discovered a plastic container labeled *Instant Glue*. Next to it sat another container: *Accelerator For Use With Instant Glue*. It made him feel dizzy, the same way he had felt the day he realized that all the *maximum* speed signs had become *minimum* speed signs and everyone knew it except him.

Looking warily in both directions, he poked a hesitant fender out of his parking space – a black BMW chased him back, its outraged, Teutonic horn condemning his timing, his driving, his very use of the pavement. It seemed to Fenton that driving had become a series of close calls and near misses, traffic rushing past him so fast that he occasionally had the sensation of having missed a shift and ending up in neutral. He feared being buried under a cascading crest of on-rushing humanity.

Fenton was convinced that this manic rush for ever-increasing speed and activity was also responsible for another disturbing trend: the transmogrification of perfectly good nouns into active verbs of dubious pedigree — activity *uber alles!* He lamented the affect of this inexorable acceleration on his beloved English language.

Fenton was not, however, a lingual Luddite. He tried hard to learn the word-forms of the nineties, introducing words

46

like accessing and scrolling, into his conversation whenever possible, but he could not yet bring himself to *like* these words. And this day was particularly disturbing.

That morning he had read an advertisement for a local copy shop called Kinko's in which they claimed to have invented *a new way to office*. The phrase had almost ruined his breakfast, but now he felt hungry again — so he decided to car downtown and find a nice place to food.

Three in a Drawer

L ate last night, sitting at my computer, waiting for my muse to come back from her break, I heard little voices, little paper-thin voices coming from inside my desk. I bent my head down and listened.

∼

"Why are you crying?"

"Because I hate my life, just lying here."

"I imagine it hurt your feelings when the boss stuck you away in this drawer."

"Hurt? My feelings are shredded. I'm a poem and poems are really nothing *but* feelings, right out to our frazzled edges. And he just stuck me in this drawer without even sending me out."

"He never sent you out?"

"Guess he got tired of me. I remember how it used to be. Late at night, he would spread me across his screen, add commas, take them out again, adjust my line breaks — but one night he just printed me out and stuck me in this drawer. I don't even know if I'm still in his computer."

"Don't give up. There's always a chance he'll pull you out, work you over, you might even end up getting published. I've heard of that happening."

"I doubt it. He took one of my best lines and gave it to some stupid short story."

"Careful, I'm a short story myself."

"Yeah? Well the worst thing is, *that* stupid story got published — one of those literary magazines, you know, with a readership of about six."

"Tell me, what's your title?"

"Well, I used to be called 'September Storm,' but one more image-ectomy and who knows what I'll be about?"

"I like that title."

"You like it? How about this? 'The lumpy slate sky goes flat and sea-birds play in slicing silhouette'?"

"I like that too."

"Yeah? Well that's the line the boss stole and gave to that short story. Now I just lie here and listen to him typing on someone else. It's really hard."

"I know what you're going through."

"How would you know? You're not a poem."

"No, but short stories have feelings too, ya' know."

"Really? How can you tell with all those extra words in the way?"

"Please — not all short stories have a lot of extra words. Some of us are quite clean and uncluttered and have important things to say."

"Then how come you're in the drawer?"

"It's the boss. He doesn't have a clue about where to send me. It's always these prissy little *anthologies of art, prose, and poetry*. I'm too powerful for them, too full of hidden meanings and subtle metaphors. He never tries Esquire, The New Yorker."

"The New Yorker? You think he should send you to the New Yorker? Let me ask you something. What's your title?"

"The Sawmill."

"And are you about a Sawmill?"

"Well ... yeah."

"And that's why you'll never get in the New Yorker. The title of a story must never have anything to do with what's in the story. That's their first rule."

"I didn't know that."

"It's true. Now, let me hear a couple of your lines."

"Okay. How about 'The machines, big as Volkswagen buses, wind up to speed, claiming every cubic inch of this hard-edged industrial space. Racing dust impregnates the sunlight, sharpening it into angled shafts of hazy brightness'."

"Hold it! Hold it! That's what you call 'a couple of lines'?"

"Yes."

"Sometimes the boss really piles on the words, doesn't he?"

"You think some of that should be cut?"

"Most of it."

"You've got to be kidding!" said a voice from the bottom of the drawer. "There aren't nearly *enough* words in that thing you just read — not enough to show anything at all!"

"What?"

"Who the hell are you?"

"I'm a novel. The boss started me six times — been lying here ever since — and, as a novel, I'd say that scene with the machines is about twenty pages too short."

"You think so?"

"Definitely. Too sketchy. Hardly tells anything. Who threw the switch? Why? What are the machines doing? What's the name of the company? Who owns it? What year is it?"

"C'mon. None of that stuff matters in this story."

"Of course it matters. It all matters. Everything matters. If you don't tell it all, there will be holes in the story and the reader will fall through."

"Isn't the reader supposed to use his imagination, fill in the spaces to suit himself?"

"Imagination! Imagination!! Gimme a break. If *anyone* out there had any imagination at all — the readers, the publishers — if any of them had the slightest scrap of imagination, the three of us wouldn't be lying here in the dark now, would we?"

Bike

He had never been good at physics and now the final exam was proving to be a total snowstorm. He had read the same paragraph over and over, but the words refused to rise up off the page and form concepts. He flicked back to the previous page, but the print lay pressed down and inscrutable as if embedded in the paper. Punctuation marks rushed past like blank signposts. He felt his brain vibrating. A high whistle that sounded like quitting time at a distant factory crowded his ears and made him dizzy.

Mike Flynn pushed himself away from his desk, away from his exam papers, and walked out — out of the Department of Physical Sciences and out through the front gate of the Allegheny Institute of Technology. That afternoon he pulled a discarded balloon-tired Schwinn bicycle from a debris box, climbed aboard, and pedaled out of town. The logical, soothing rhythm flowed up through his body. The bike became his companion, his home, and he became Bike Flynn.

Standing on the pedals, Bike squeezed altitude out of his rusted machine.

As he forced his way up the hill, a sudden flurry of metallic flashes and jungle-bird colors burst from behind him and flowed past on both sides; bicycles — thin-tired, silent, and climbing at twice the speed of the Schwinn. The riders wore impossibly bright clothing so tight as to be painted on their skin and little helmets like slices of colored watermelon. Bike watched them flow gently up the hill and become smaller and smaller until, reaching the crest, they dropped out of sight, bicycles first, then their shirts, and finally their funny-shaped hats.

An eighteen-wheeler roared past, shifting gears, gaining speed, and trailing a spinning wake of dirty air. Bike swerved behind the truck, then recovered. He waved a fist at the receding silver rectangle.

"You son'bitches gonna' kill us yet." He glared down at the Schwinn. "Goddamn it, Rusty! If you could move like those skinny-assed bikes, those son'bitch trucks wouldn't be able to catch up with us!" He reached back with his leg and gave the rear tire a kick with the side of his foot. Then he sat back for the cooling glide down into town.

The first place he went was to the post office, rode right in the front door and down the hall to his postal box. The clerk leaned over the counter, looked at the dusty tire tracks, and went back to work.

Bike opened the box and extracted two envelopes. The Department of Social Services mailed him a check every month because they thought he was crazy. His parents sent checks, for the same reason. After a stop at the bank, he leaned the Schwinn against a tree and walked into a shop with a bicycle-shaped sign that read: *The Village Peddler*.

Inside, a young man was tuning a wheel as if it were a musical instrument, tapping and listening as he tightened each spoke. The paint on the new bikes gleamed like bright melted glass. Their tires looked like rubber worms with tiny black treads.

"How fast does this one go?" Bike asked.

"Depends on how fast you peddle."

Bike thought about that for a while. "Does it go up hills easy?"

"Depends on what gear you're in." The young man continued to tune.

"How many gears has it got?"

"Twenty-seven."

"Don't bullshit me, man! I want to buy one of these things."

The young man put down the wheel and came to the front of the shop. "It has twenty-seven gears."

"Really? How do you shift 'em?"

"This lever operates the derailleur for the crank set, this one's for the cassette."

"How do you know where to put the levers?" Bike asked.

"You choose the proper sprocket ratio."

"Uh?"

"Yeah. Bike speed is a function of pedal speed and pedal pressure is determined by the relative size of the sprockets. Basic physics."

Bike felt a familiar vibration in his head.

"Of course, if you increase the length of the crank arm," the young man continued, "the moment of force increases and you get more torque; the law of the lever."

"Oh . . . yeah."

Out in the sunshine, Bike pulled the Schwinn upright and threw his leg across the worn leather seat. "Guess it's you and me, Rusty. Those new bikes look good, but they're jam-packed with physics and you know how I feel about physics."

A Visit to the Truth

"You look beautiful, just beautiful. Your face has more color, you look happier, really, and you look so much better than the last time I was here."

She smiles, but doesn't turn her head in my direction. Her wheelchair is pushed up close to the table.

She does not really look better. She looks smaller and her eyes have lost some brightness. She also moves more slowly than when I visited her a month ago.

"We should have you out of here in no time, back in your apartment, cooking for your friends, just like before."

I am helping my mother to eat her lunch, guiding her shiny, wrinkled fingers with my hand. Her sight is dim. She smells of talcum and shampoo. Food odors flow past, but mostly the cavernous room holds the plastic smell of indoor-outdoor carpeting.

Together we are stabbing rubber rectangles of ham and pieces of macaroni, loading her fork for the shaky journey to her mouth. She opens her mouth wider than necessary and moves her jaw slowly. She leans close and speaks into my ear.

"I imagine you will want to go out after this and get yourself a real meal."

"No, not really. I love the food here. Tastes like you have a really fine chef, better than a lot of the restaurants I eat in."

~

The dining room is mostly white. The painted green trim has the hand-brushed feeling of a community center or a summer camp. Peruvian Lilies bloom on a water-ringed plant stand by the door. The twelve-foot ceiling makes the diners and the furniture look smaller than they really are.

"This place is just beautiful, everything about it," I tell her.

"It is, isn't it," she says, staring out into her private blurry space. "I want you to meet Mary." My mother's arm makes a small, vague motion toward the other side of the table as if brushing aside a curtain. She has lost more sight than she wants me to know.

The other person at our table is an ancient, beautiful woman with tissue-paper wrinkles on her neck and clear, bird-like eyes. She has been watching me like a tiny hawk.

"Hello, I'm Mary."

I nod and smile back.

"I don't usually sit here. I usually sit alone. I like to sit alone." She waits for a moment, then looks from me to my mother who is bending forward, her fork click clicking against the flowered plate as she pursues a slippery disc of zucchini off the edge and onto the tablecloth where it flops down like a flaccid green coin. I help her to stab the zucchini and ask Mary why she eats alone.

"Chatterers. Good conversation is fine, but I can't abide chattering. But I don't *always* eat alone. Right now I'm sitting with my friend Joan here." She nods toward my mother. My mother's name is Kathleen.

My mother looks up brightly and says, "Isn't it wonderful? We can sit anywhere we want. The waiters bring the food to wherever we are."

As far as I can tell, *one* waiter is serving the entire room, a quick man with a Brooklyn accent and skin the color of bittersweet chocolate.

"When I lived in southern California," says Mary, "I could see the ocean from my deck and there were always a lot of people around. Everyone was rich." She waits.

"That's a good situation to be in," I reply.

"Mostly people from the studio."

"You were in the film industry?"

"A little." She smiles and looks away, then turns back. The smile is gone. "But my son didn't like any of them."

"He didn't like your friends?"

"Yes, uh, no. He did terrible things when they came to visit—kicked their dogs, let air out of their tires. Once he set fire to a man's luggage." Her head moves in recollected bafflement, slowly, from side to side. "And then he would tell the most outrageous lies about what had happened."

My mother laughs and says, "That sounds awful." Mary frowns. I feel bad for Mary and am tempted to rescue her. I *do* rescue her; I make an excuse for her son.

"Probably just a phase. I did things like that when I was a kid." I hesitate, and then plunge ahead, looking down at my mother. "Do you remember when the Rose Cottage burned down?" I ask her.

"I do," she says immediately. "That was the prettiest guesthouse on the estate, all those rose bushes around it, and that beautiful wood paneling inside. A damn shame." Now my mother is frowning and Mary looks interested.

"Well, I've never told you this before," I say to my mother, "but I was the one who set that fire."

I feel as if someone else were speaking, each word tumbling one after another out of a dark mist. I'm not hitting her with the words, just allowing them to hang in the air after sixty years. I feel my throat get hard and wonder if it is possible to be *in trouble* with someone who is ninety-eight years old and dying. My mother rests her warm, soft hand on my arm.

"No, dear. You didn't start that fire. Don't you remember? It was the boys from down the hill." She leans toward Mary, her little hand pressing my arm more firmly. "I'm just so grateful to have a son who always tells the truth." She looks up at me and smiles into my face. "He's such an honest little boy."

The Duplex

In the early sixties, when the San Francisco flower children were in bloom and most of the country was looking west, our little family decided to move to the Bay Area. We made a plan. My new wife and her eight-year-old daughter would stay in NYC until the school year ended; I would come out ahead of them and find us a place to live.

Housing, it turned out, was scarce, and as the school year drew to a close, I was getting desperate. Then, one morning, a classified ad caught my attention.

> FOR RENT
> SAUSALITO DUPLEX
> D DOCK – SLIP A

I headed north. In Sausalito a young nautical type carrying a sail bag came along and I caught his eye.

"D dock around here?" I asked.

"The only dock farther up the bay is that place with the trees." He pointed with his chin. "Don't know what they call it. It's just a barge and a couple of fish boats."

A yellow clay road, rutted and pot-holed, led north for several hundred yards, then widened at the end and quit. A few cars sat facing in different directions as if trying to figure out where the road had gone. A hand-painted sign, *D Dock – Yacht Owners and Their Guests Only*, hung on a bent nail pounded into a tree.

A gangway with no hand rails reached down from the embankment. A weathered wooden barge lay alongside the dock. On the deck of the barge stood a large cobbled-together shed built out of scrap wood and sheet metal using a lot more imagination than talent. Its bright orange walls glowed in the sunlight. I walked down onto the dock. The tide was dropping. The barge rested hard aground and salt water poured out of large holes in the hull where marine borers had left the wood looking like sponge cake. The lip-curling smell of rotting wetness drifted out of the bilge.

On the deck of the barge, a husky man with bushy eyebrows and a rusted-Brillo beard dozed on a kitchen chair tipped back against the shed. A small dog lay nearby with his head hanging over the side of the barge, watching a nervous herring in a draining puddle of salt water. The man opened his eyes and nodded as I approached.

"Excuse me," I said. "I'm looking for D dock, Slip A."

"Well, you found it," he said, riding the chair forward and resting his hands on his knees.

"I saw this ad in the paper. It says there's supposed to be a duplex apartment around here." The man smiled and nodded. The dog barked as the trapped fish became a flurry of fins and tail.

"You're in the right place," the man said. "This is the duplex." Hand open, palm up, he indicated the orange shed as if he were making a presentation. "I live in this half," he said, "the other half is for rent. Both units have wood stoves and windows looking out across the bay. C'mon aboard."

I reached up for a handshake. He bent forward, took my hand, and, in one powerful motion, lifted me up onto the deck, giving the hand a shake before letting go. "Russo," he said. "Frank Russo, Harbor Master and owner of this barge. Take a look inside."

He led me into a cavernous box with a low ceiling. A row of glass doors had been nailed together to make a window-wall and a pot-bellied stove as big as a water heater lurked in one corner. Daylight shone in where the stove pipe had been poked through the corrugated steel roof.

"Build to suit," he said, "any way you want. I can start on it tomorrow."

"What else are you going to do to it?" I asked, looking around for evidence of a kitchen, a bathroom, things like that.

"Anything you want. This place will be like heaven. Let me show you how nice *my* place is."

He led the way along the deck, past piles of scrap wood and assorted debris, until we came to an opening at the other end of the shed. The uneven floor was covered by a pale-green carpet. A mattress with a sleeping bag lay in one corner and a single wooden shelf ran along three walls apparently holding everything Mr. Russo owned. A green garden hose entered through a hole in the roof and, supported by rusty nails, traced the edge of the ceiling until, like an emaciated jungle snake, its head drooped down into a chipped white sink.

Russo watched me as I looked around the room. My face must have told him something.

"Simple, I like to keep it simple," he said quickly. He walked over to the windows. "This view. You ever see anything like it?"

He offered me some wine. I said yes because it was turning into that kind of a day.

I sat down at the table. Russo took down two glasses and rinsed them with the hose nozzle. Water drained out of the sink and fell directly through a hole in the floor without the aid of hose or pipe. We talked our way through the bottle of wine and stared out the window. He rolled a joint. We spoke of life, what we owned, what owned us, and what we planned to do about it.

The tide continued to fall until we were surrounded by gray-green mud, gently uneven, almost puffy like the surface of some soggy planet pushing up from beneath. The eucalyptus trees chopped up the sunlight, dappling it across the deck and into the room. A long-legged white bird with a scraggle of black feathers on the back of its head, moved past with silent care, leaving a double row of wishbone footprints in a gently meandering line. The world shone bright as a schoolboy's Saturday morning, rich with positive expectation.

I could see San Francisco in the distance and possibilities all around.

My Guitar Gently Weeps

Some of us have a great life and don't even recognize it. Take for instance the hundreds of items hanging from the ceiling, resting on shelves, or laid out in the windows of this pawn shop. This is heaven; but there's always somebody moaning and groaning about something.

"He used to love me, how can he leave me in a place like this!?

"It's so insulting. I'm worth thousands of dollars and people offer ten bucks!"

But you'll never hear me complain. I'm a guitar, one of many hanging peacefully up here on the back wall. My strings may be a little stretched out and I haven't seen my case in a couple of years, but I know what it's like out there in the real world and I really can't understand the constant bitching.

And you know who bitch the worst? The damned carvedback instruments. We guitars sometimes hang here for years without saying a word, but if a violin or a viola gets hung up here, you aught to hear them piss and moan. Those squeaky voices are enough to loosen your goddamned frets. Just because their owners hold them under their chins and against their cheeks, they think there's some kind of a love affair going on or something and then they can't believe it when they end up in a pawn shop. There was a cello in here a while back who said his owner held him between her legs when she played him. His poor maple heart was just broken when she put him in here for fifty dollars. His strings vibrated in a low moan for two days. Then he just split right down the back and his sound post fell out and rolled across the floor. The most heart-wrenching part was the way he crunched and twanged when the boss threw him in the debris box.

Me, I'd much rather be in here than on the outside. Yeah, maybe the dust does get kinda thick, especially hanging up here by the ceiling, but at least the roof doesn't leak. I'd rather be dusty than wet any day. We guitars don't do too well with wet. See this place on my neck where the varnish is wrinkled? A leaky goddamned roof. And it isn't the wrinkles I mind so much, but when the water gets into your wood, the next thing you know you've got glue problems. That's what most guitars die from, ya' know. It's a very painful condition. One time I had to have my whole sound board cut off and glued back on after one of my owners got drunk and took me in the shower with him. I've never sounded the same since.

It's like I always say, they stroke you with their finger tips and brag about your varnish, but when they're hungry, they'll pawn you without even thinking twice.

I remember when I was first built. The old Mexican guy who glued me up handled me as if I were glass. When he put on my first strings and tuned them like angel voices, he played me so pretty I figured I was headed for Carnegie Hall. But I ended up in a music store in LA..

I can hardly remember how many owners I've had — beginners who never ever could get me in tune, college kids with grips like cable-car brakes, cowboys who knew four chords, and rock-and-rollers who knew three. One folk singer was pretty good at finger picking and I remember a jazz player who got my hopes up for a while, but most of them were strummers and thumpers who left me out-of-tune and gathering dust for years at a time and mostly used me to play the one tune they knew to impress girls. At least in this place I get out of my case and have a chance to show off my grain and flash my shiny varnish around. So, like I said, I love it here. The only time I worry is when someone lifts me down, brushes his fingernails across my strings, and asks, "How much do you want for this one?"

Dibbs

The three of us were walking home from school in single file because the shortcut is narrow and we didn't want to get poked by the blackberry bushes. Hank was in front. He's always in front 'cause he's in the seventh grade. I'm in the sixth. Ginny's only in the fourth.

Each of us was looking in a different direction. Hank was strolling along, staring up into the sky like he's trying to sneak up on God or something. I was looking where I was going, straight ahead, like a normal person, and Ginny was looking down at the ground. When she was little, she stepped in dog poop. That's why she always looks down at the ground when she walks. And that's the reason Ginny was the one who spotted the two perfect circles half hidden in the dirt at the edge of the path—two shiny quarters.

She yelled "Dibbs!!" and we all stopped. She scooped up the quarters and held them out flat on her hand, blowing off the dust. Hank leaned over, lifted the coins from her palm, and rattled them in his fist like a pair of dice.

"What are we gonna' buy?" he asked.

Ginny's voice came quick and loud. "What do ya mean, we? Give it back! I called Dibbs!"

"Take it easy. I'm just holding 'em so no one comes along and steals 'em."

Ginny jumped up and down like a puppy. "C'mon, give

'em back!"

Hank suggested we buy cigarettes.

"No way!" Ginny yelled. "We don't even smoke!"

Hank looked down at her and spoke softly. "How do you know you don't smoke? Maybe you really love to smoke but you don't even know it because you never tried."

"I found 'em so I decide what to buy — and I'm gonna' get a charm bracelet I saw at Woolworth's. It's twenty five cents. The rest I'm gonna spend on candy-corn and ju-jubes."

"I think that God really meant for *me* to find the money," Hank said slowly, as if it were being divinely revealed to him at that very moment. He rattled the coins in his hand.

"Uh Uh!" Ginny yelled. "Whoever calls Dibbs gets it. That's the rules!"

"No, really, listen," Hank continued. I expected to hear choirs of angels, but all we got was more talk. "It's only logical," he said. "God had me walking in front so that I'd find the money. He obviously meant for *me* to have it, but I just wasn't paying attention."

"That's dumb," Ginny said. "You both stepped right over?"

Hank hooked a thumb in my direction. "He was God's second choice, but he wasn't paying attention either." Hank looked down at Ginny. "You were just lucky — and luck isn't as important as what God wants." Hank's family is Roaming Catholic so I guess that's why God always seems to ends up on Hank's side.

The street lights came on and we still hadn't figured out what to buy. Hank said he'd take care of the money and that tomorrow we should meet in the same place after school and decide. Ginny told him all seventh graders are jerks and we went home.

The next afternoon, Hank and I got to the shortcut first and poked around in the yellow dust to see if there were any more quarters. Then we saw Frankie Paterno coming down the path. Frankie was an eighth grader and the toughest kid in the school. He was staring at the ground, kicking the dust. He looked up quick like he was surprised to see us. Then Ginny arrived.

"Hi, Frankie," Ginny said. "Looking for something?"

"Yeah," he said. "I lost some money, two quarters, right here." He scowled at each of us.

"I don't have any money," I said, holding out both hands, palms up.

Ginny said "Neither do I." We were all looking at Hank.

Frankie pushed past me and Ginny and stood in front of Hank.

"Give it!" he said.

Hank started to say, "Finder keepers, losers weep ... " but Frankie grabbed the front of his shirt.

"It's gonna' be finders sleepers if you don't give it!" he shouted into Hank's face.

Hank dug into his pocket and handed over the quarters. Frankie grabbed the money and was gone.

At lunch the next day, Ginny was wearing a new charm bracelet and Frankie Paterno was eating ju-jubes.

Nobody ever mentioned the money again and, of course, no one ever forgot the power of Dibbs.

The Toast

An afternoon breeze curled back the pale yellow curtains, Palm-tree shadows flickered on the white wall beside the bed, and somewhere a mariachi band was playing. Terry and I had spent our siesta making love and had fallen asleep, slippery and folded together, wrapped in the tossed and wrinkled sheets. I don't remember how long we slept.

She knew I was awake before I knew it. She smiled when I opened my eyes, resting her head on my chest. I loved Terry very much and making love to her had lost none of its joyous magic, but I awoke to an aching sadness and discovered I was fighting back tears.

The reason for this trip, this week by the ocean in Mexico, was to focus on each other and perhaps rekindle a flame. Maybe we were fooling ourselves. Maybe the only flames that reignite themselves are joke candles on birthday cakes.

"Tell me about the first woman you were in love with," Terry said.

"Why?"

"Just curious." I kissed the top of her head.

"It wasn't a woman," I said, waiting and letting the possibilities suggest themselves. "It was a girl. I was in the fifth grade."

"Do you remember her name?"

"Lorraine Kennedy."

"Was she Irish?"

"Very Irish. She had green eyes, a laugh like the tinkle of wind chimes, and her hair smelled like Prell. She sat at the desk in front of me."

"You still love her?"

"Some part of me does, I guess."

Terry looked up. "Is that how it works?" she asked, "we go along leaving little parts of ourselves here and there and we never get them back?"

"Maybe, I don't know."

Terry rolled to the edge of the bed and swung her legs down. She ran her fingers through her hair, brushing it back, the angled sunshine silhouetting her perfect breast against the plaster wall. She touched my hand and went into the shower.

Later, in the early evening, as the sun began to stretch the shadows and the sky took on a pale orange wash, we sat at a palapa by the beach drinking tequila.

"Why did you ask me about Lorraine?" I asked.

"Lorraine?"

"Lorraine Kennedy."

"Oh ... yeah." Terry gazed out past the sand, past the surf, out toward the crisp, red horizon. She was quiet for a while. When she spoke she was still looking at the ocean. "Last week," she said, "just before we left for this trip, I got a call from an old friend. God, I hadn't thought about him in years. We dated in college."

"The first boy you were in love with?"

Terry looked down and pushed sand with her toe. She didn't say anything.

"You plan to see him again?" I asked.

"Yes, I think so. I want to see if he's still like I remember him."

~

We flew home the next day. Then life flowed in and washed us apart. Terry started dating her college friend and I started waiting to heal. Things were pretty scratchy for a while. I was drag-yourself-around, middle-of-the-bed lonely — the kind of lonely that changes the color of the sunlight and makes rooms seem bigger and emptier.

Then, the other day, just as I was starting to come alive again, I ran into Terry at the car wash. She kissed my cheek, told me she was getting married. I told her I was happy to hear that and she invited me to this reception, this bouncing, pink and white party where we are right now. I'm really glad to be here. The champagne is good and getting better by the glass — everyone looks so all dressed up, so full of celebration — me too — life is good, really, like the champagne — everyone at this whirling, laughing party is beautiful, everyone is saying the right things, everybody is exactly who they are supposed to be and doing what they are supposed to be doing — but my lips feel a little numb and the floor's going soft under my feet so I think I'll have another champagne to clear my head.

I see Terry and her new husband — they look sculpted and scrubbed and impossibly joyful — I decide to propose a toast, yes, yes, just the right thing, a toast! — so I tap on my glass with a knife (ting, ting, ting) and people hear me doing it and they start tapping on their glasses (ting, ting, ting, ting) until the talking dries up and the room fills with quiet — I announce to all the expectant eyes, announce a lot louder than I mean to, that I'd like to propose a toast to this perfect couple — the newlyweds smile and raise their glasses to receive the toast — the words of the toast are still organizing themselves in my mind, so I smile and reach out with my glass to touch theirs — the words should be along any minute now.

But, unexpectedly, the room takes a dip and a spin — I do a little stutter step to the left, grabbing for the edge of the table — my out-stretched arm holds my glass, swings it around, and there is an explosion of champagne and crystal as if their goblets had been sparkling piniatas — the shards like diamonds spread across the table cloth and people stand quickly, dabbing at their clothes with napkins — the room vibrates in tense silence for a moment . . . then people roll their eyes away, the music and conversation start up again, and the party regains its footing.

I want to shout to the crowd, "Wait! Wait! I haven't given my toast yet!" but I don't shout — I don't say anything — I guess I've already said it — I guess that was it, my toast to the perfect couple from the very very bottom of my heart.

Detour

My father bought an old Airstream motor home, tossed some things into it, including me, and we rolled down the eastern slope of the Rockies, south through Colorado, and out onto the New Mexico desert like a big, silver bowling ball.

The real estate man had told him it was desert and desert was what he wanted; he bought sixty acres. Now it was time to visit "the property." I was twelve and game for anything.

On the back of the road map, I read some interesting facts about desert animals and the unique ways they have learned to survive; insects that dig into solid rock, frogs in suspended animation. Right away I could see we were into something different, something big.

On the pencil-straight highway, I gazed out the side window, watching the foreground spin past like the edge of a giant turntable. Puffy white clouds huddled around distant mesas like sheep at a salt lick; the cloud shadows burned patches on the sand. In the evenings, after the orange glow had faded, the desert seemed to shrink and grow at the same time; cozy in the reaching headlights, yet stretching out forever. A million stars vibrated like jumbled pinholes in the black drape of the night.

Approaching Santa Fe in late afternoon, Dad slowed down to read a sign propped against a fence post: "LAST GAS FOR 200 MILES — TURN LEFT A HUNDRED AND FIFTY FEET."

He checked the gauge, braked, and turned. A half-mile down a dirt road we found a leaning wooden shed with TEXACO on the roof. A hand-painted sign said *camping*. A large man with mirrored sunglasses and Harley tattoos on both arms sat in the doorway. We climbed down and dad asked, "Want to fill 'er up?"

The man shifted a toothpick from one side of his mouth to the other, smiled, and said, "Nope."

My dad looked puzzled. "You mean you're out of gas?"

The man smiled again. "Nope."

"Then what's the problem?"

"You ain't signed in yet."

"Sign? For gasoline?"

"Nope." The toothpick went back to the other side. "You gotta sign for camping, state law."

"But we're not camping here."

"Oh," said the man, leaning back in his chair. "How much gas you got in that thing?"

"About a quarter tank."

"Guess you'll be wantin' to sign in then." The sign-in book rasped across the grit on the counter as he pushed it across. "Forty bucks a night, two night minimum."

My dad blinked. "I just need enough gas to get to Fulton."

"Sorry. The gasoline's reserved for our guests — so's the water. Anyhow, this place here is jus' as good as this Fulton place you're lookin' for. They're all the same. Everything's the same out here, same for five hundred miles in every direction — so it don't really *matter* where you are."

"It matters to me. We own sixty acres near Fulton, but we can't find Fulton on the map."

"You own it and you don't know where it is?"

"Fulton. It's near Socorro."

"This Fulton place anywhere near Bromley?"

"Bromley. Bromley." My dad's finger pounced from place to place on the map. "I don't see Bromley either."

"Too bad," said the man. "I *know* where Bromley is."

"Near Socorro?"

"Nope, Bromley's a good three hundred miles east of here. You'd never make it on a quarter tank." My dad stepped back and looked over at me, confused. I shrugged.

The next morning, after sleeping behind the man's shed and paying for a tank of gas plus the eighty-dollar minimum, we were on the road again. Almost immediately, a Chevron station loomed on the left, Rotten Robbie on the right.

My father smiled. "Like it says on the map, desert animals devise unique ways to survive."

The Pickup

Ten miles east of Memphis, Hank Nelson's truck quit at sixty miles an hour, headlights, engine, and all. He swung the pickup around the dark curve, and rolled to a stop on the shoulder. A finger-nail of a moon gave him enough light to do the things the auto-ignorant always do when their cars stop running — raise the hood, tap the air filter, wiggle the wires, but nothing worked. Hank swore and reached across for his guitar. He climbed out, sat on the tailgate, and began running through the chords of a song he'd been working on.

Back through the oaks and alders that lined both sides of the road came a flicker of light, a car, its high beams jumping and flashing among the trunks of the trees. The lights swung round the bend and caught Hank, the pickup, and a quarter mile of highway in blinding, blue-white brightness. The car stopped some distance behind the truck and Hank walked back toward it, his guitar in one hand, shading his eyes with the other. All he could see were the headlights and an armada of flying insects throwing themselves at the lenses and spiraling off into the darkness. Another step forward, out of the glare, and he could see that the car was actually a big, serious-looking passenger van with dark tinted windows, tires half as tall as his pickup, and a record-company logo painted on the side. The driver was a woman. The hot Tennessee night had textured the front of the vehicle with flattened insects and the highway had powdered it with dust.

The driver opened her window. "Outa' gas?"

"Don't think so. Filled her up back in Memphis."

"You got any tools?" she asked.

Recovering from the glare, Hank could see the woman more clearly now. Short black curls framed her face and, a smile played around the edges of her mouth when she spoke.

"Not sure tools would do me any good," Hank answered. "I don't know beans about cars."

She laughed. "Boy, you guys are a stitch. My ex husband was like that." She looked down at Hank's guitar. "And musicians are the worst. All they know is music. They're lucky if they can tie their own shoes."

"Your ex husband a musician by any chance?"

"Afraid so."

Hank felt his outa-luck feeling begin to fade. She had a sparkle about her and intelligent eyes. "This a band truck?" he asked.

"You guessed it." She hooked a thumb toward the back of the van. "Full of sleeping musicians." She opened the door, climbed down, and lit a cigarette. "What puts a helpless boy like you out in the woods in the middle of the night?" she asked.

"Coming home from work. I play weekends at The River Inn in Memphis."

"The restaurant?"

"Yeah."

"Nobody listens, right?"

"You got it."

"That's why we don't play those places anymore," she said. "We used to, but now we only play clubs and concerts."

"You the singer?" he asked.

"No, I just drive, help set up the stand, stuff like that."

Hank wondered how successful a band had to be to afford a roadie like her. He stepped back to read the lettering on the side of the van — The Stoney Mountain Boys.

"Wow!" Hank said. "The Stoney Mountain Boys. I caught them in Knoxville last year. That's a hell of a band. I never heard pickin' like that.

"Yeah, they're good." She walked over to Hank's pickup and sat on the tail gate next to him. "I been driving seven hours," she said. "Feels good to take a break." She stretched her arms and flexed her shoulders. Hank wondered if she knew how good she looked doing that.

"How'd you get a job like this?" he asked, sitting down next to her, still holding his guitar.

"My ex husband was one of the original Stoney Mountain Boys, but he started taking the *"stoney"* part too seriously and quit the band. I found I liked the road better than I liked him so I just kept on going."

They sat quietly and listened to the tree frogs while she had another cigarette. "Name's Carla," she said.

"Hank. Hank Nelson." They shook hands.

"What do you want to do about your truck?" she asked.

Hank thought for a moment. "If you're going on through to Chattanooga and I could get a ride with you, I'll call my brother. He lives near here. He's a mechanic. He can pick up the truck in the morning."

"Great," she said. "You can spell me on the driving."

Hank grabbed his guitar case and backpack out of the pickup, climbed into the van, and away they rolled into the Tennessee night.

Hank drove first and they talked. As the sun came up, Carla took the wheel and they talked some more. "These guys really sleep," Hank said, indicating the curtained rear of the van. "I guess I should tell you the truth," she said. "There's nobody sleeping back there and I'm not going as far as Chattanooga. The band's on vacation and I'm just headin' home to Nashville for a few days."

"Really?" Hank looked across at her. "That's okay," he said. "I don't have a brother who's a mechanic."